ADAM✦SHARP
•Code Word Kangaroo•

by George Edward Stanley
illustrated by Guy Francis

A STEPPING STONE BOOK™
Random House New York

To Jennifer Arena:
Thanks for golden days past,
and here's to future random ideas!
—G.E.S.

To Bill and Bob
—G.F.

www.randomhouse.com/kids

Library of Congress Cataloging-in-Publication Data
Stanley, George Edward.
Code word kangaroo / by George Edward Stanley ; illustrated by Guy Francis. — 1st ed.
    p.   cm. — (Adam Sharp ; #6)
"A stepping stone book."
SUMMARY: Eight-year-old secret agent Adam Sharp travels to Australia where, with the assistance of Alice Springs and a washed-up TV star, he tracks down the evil mastermind behind a plan to block all television stations except his own—the Happy Channel.
ISBN 0-375-82689-0 (pbk.) — ISBN 0-375-92689-5 (lib. bdg.)
[1. Television broadcasting—Fiction. 2. Actors and actresses—Fiction. 3. Spies—Fiction. 4. Australia—Fiction.] I. Francis, Guy, ill. II. Title. III. Series: Stanley, George Edward. Adam Sharp ; v #6.
PZ7.S78694Cn 2004   [Fic]—dc22   2004000284

Printed in the United States of America   First Edition   10 9 8 7 6 5 4 3 2 1

Contents

1

The Happy Channel

It was Saturday afternoon. Adam Sharp was at his friend Clyde's house. They were playing a video game called *Pretend You're a Spy!*

"You're really good at this," Clyde said. "Are you *sure* you never played before?"

Adam shrugged. What could he say? He'd had a lot of practice, but not with this game.

Adam was a *real* spy. He worked for IM-8, the world's most secret agency. But he couldn't tell Clyde that. Then it wouldn't be a secret.

Adam zapped Clyde's last spy. "I win!" he said. "Now what do you want to do?"

Clyde switched off the video game. There was nothing on the TV screen but static. "That's weird. . . ."

He flipped from one station to another. Static, static, more static.

All of a sudden, a woman's face came on. She said, "Welcome to the Happy Channel! Here is the latest happy news."

For several minutes, Adam and Clyde

watched stories about birthday parties, new toys, junk food, and pets.

"Wow!" Clyde said. "This is great!"

Adam didn't think so. If people were too happy, they wouldn't care about bad stuff happening around them. That meant someone could take over the world!

"I have to go," Adam said. "See you later!" Adam ran out of Clyde's house and jumped on his bike. He raced toward Friendly Elementary School. When he got there, he turned the rubber grips on his handlebars two times. He heard a click from the front door. It swung open.

Halfway down the hall, Adam stopped

at the janitor's closet. He stepped inside
and pulled on a broom handle. A secret
door opened.

Adam was in IM-8 Headquarters.

T and J were watching the Happy
Channel. T was the head of IM-8. During
school days, J was a janitor. But at night,
he made all of IM-8's secret gadgets.

"You've seen it, too!" Adam cried.

"Yeah!" J said. "I really liked the show about puppy dogs. And have you checked out Happy Radio?"

"Quite good! Quite good!" T said. "Don't you agree, Sharp?"

"No, sir! I think it means *trouble,*" Adam said. "There's only one TV and radio station. Someone must be sending up evil satellites to mess up the good satellites!"

"That can't be true," T said. "There's no sign of it." He pointed to a TV screen that covered an entire wall. It showed Earth from outer space. "IM-8 keeps track of who sends up satellites," T told Adam.

Just then, a little blue satellite shot up from the middle of China. It began to orbit the Earth.

"The Chinese just launched one," T said.

After that, little blue satellites shot up from England and France.

"The British and the French are busy today, too," T said.

All of a sudden, a lot of little red circles shot up from the middle of Australia.

"What are those?" Adam asked.

"Just hot-air balloons. The Aussies started sending up a lot of them about an hour ago," T replied. "They are probably having a balloon race."

An hour ago? Adam thought. *That's when the radios and TVs stopped working.*

"Sir! I don't think it's a balloon race," Adam said. "I think it's an evil plot to take over the world! I have to go to Australia at once!"

2
Alice Springs

The IM-8 jet flew halfway around the world to Australia. It landed at a secret airport near Lake Disappointment.

Before Adam got off the plane, he checked himself in a mirror. His tuxedo was wrinkled from the long flight.

Alice Springs was standing beside an old pickup truck. Alice was IM-8's agent in Australia. She had on a tan shirt and green shorts. Her hat brim curled up on one side, Aussie-style.

"G'day!" Adam said. During missions, he always spoke the language of the country he was working in.

"G'day to you, Sharp!" Alice said.

Adam looked at the dry grass, the thornbushes, and the kangaroos that were hopping around. "So this is the famous Outback," he said.

Alice nodded. "What's left of it, mate," she said sadly.

Adam frowned. "What do you mean?"

"See that fence over there?" Alice asked.

Adam looked. "The one that's fifty feet tall and has razor blades, electric wire, and security cameras on top of it?"

"That's the one," Alice said. "Well, now the Outback only goes from here to there."

Adam was stunned. "I thought the Outback was the size of Alaska," he said.

"It used to be, mate," Alice said. "Then

a rich sheep rancher bought it and put up that fence."

"Wow! It must be the biggest sheep ranch in the world!" Adam said.

"People from Australia aren't allowed in there anymore," Alice said. "But the sheep make a lot of noise. There must be millions and millions. Sometimes you can hear them baaing all the way to Sydney!"

"We have to get inside!" Adam told Alice what he had seen on the TV screen at IM-8 Headquarters. "The hot-air balloons are coming from the ranch. We need to find out who is flying them and why!"

"It can't be done, mate. The security is

too good," Alice said. "We'd never make it over that fence."

Just then, more kangaroos hopped by. One by one, they jumped over the tall fence.

"They really jump high," Adam said.

Alice nodded.

Adam turned away from the kangaroos. "There must be some way that we can get onto that ranch," he said. He thought hard.

Another kangaroo hopped by. It jumped over the tall fence, too.

"Of course!" Adam cried. "That's it!"

3
The Missing Sheep

"Our mission is Code Word Kangaroo," Adam said. "We're going to ride kangaroos over that fence!"

Alice's eyes got wide. "Jolly *jumbuck*, mate! That's a brilliant idea!" she said.

Adam agreed. "But how will we catch them?" he asked.

"Oh, that's easy," Alice said.

Two kangaroos were hopping toward the fence. Alice ran over and stood in front of them.

"Alice!" Adam cried. "You'll be crushed!"

Alice didn't move. Instead, she pointed a finger at the kangaroos. She stared deep into their eyes.

The kangaroos stopped. They stood as still as statues.

"Wow!" Adam said. "What did you do?"

"I hypnotized them," Alice said.

"I looked at your file before I left," Adam said. "There was nothing in it about that."

Alice shrugged. "I didn't think IM-8 would care," she said.

"Alice, IM-8 needs people who can do that," Adam said. "You never know when we'll have to hypnotize an animal during a mission."

"Oops," Alice said.

Adam and Alice each climbed on a kangaroo's back. Alice snapped her fingers. The kangaroos woke up and started hopping again.

Right before they reached the tall fence, the kangaroos leaped high into the air. They barely cleared the razor blades and the electric wire. When they landed on the other side, Adam and Alice jumped off.

For the next few hours, they hiked across the Outback.

They saw snakes.

They saw scorpions.

They saw dingoes.

But they didn't see any sheep. Or hot-air
balloons.

"We need to make camp," Adam said. He
didn't want to tell Alice, but his feet hurt.
His shiny black shoes pinched like crazy.

Just then, they heard some loud baaing.

"Sheep!" Alice said. "Behind that big
thornbush!"

The thornbush had long, sharp thorns.

"Alice, maybe that's why we didn't see them," Adam said. "They're stuck!"

But when Adam and Alice got to the bush, there were no sheep anywhere.

"Where did they go?" Alice said.

"They didn't go anywhere," Adam said. He carefully pulled apart the branches of the thornbush. "Look—a loudspeaker! That's where the baaing was coming from. Alice, there are no sheep on this sheep ranch!"

4
Wayne Wallaby,
Snake Hunter

Adam and Alice heard another noise.

"Someone's coming!" Adam said.

They hid behind the thornbush.

Minutes later, an old motorcycle with a sidecar pulled up. It stopped beside another thornbush. A man got off and looked around.

"That bloke looks familiar," Alice said.

Just then, the man said, "This place is as fine as frog's hair!"

Alice grabbed Adam's arm. "I know that voice!" she said.

The man took a spotlight and a movie camera out of the sidecar and set them up. Then he got down on the ground and started crawling toward the camera.

"I'm flat-out like a lizard drinkin'," the man said. "Over behind that thornbush is one of the most dangerous snakes in Australia. A three-fanged whippersnapper! One bite from it, and I'm dead!"

Alice stood up. "It's Wayne Wallaby, snake hunter!" she cried. She started running toward the man. "Wayne! Wayne!"

"Alice! Stop! You broke an IM-8 rule!" Adam hissed. "Never—"

Alice reached the man and said, "Wayne! Mr. Wallaby, can I have your autograph?"

"Abso-blooming-lutely!" Wayne said.

"I watched Wayne's show all the time before it went off the air," Alice told Adam.

"I guess the Happy Channel put a lot of people out of work," Adam said.

"It wasn't that, mate," Wayne said. "I lost my touch. The snakes started biting me."

"I read about that," Alice said. "I hope you're okay now." She patted his arm.

"Ouch!" Wayne said.

"Why are you here, Wayne?" Adam asked.

"My TV days are over, mate. I'm making a movie instead," Wayne told him. "That rancher fenced in the dangerous snakes, so I dug a tunnel under the fence and rode my motorcycle through."

Adam was impressed. He wished he'd thought of that.

"Oh, Wayne! Can I be in your movie?" Alice said. "I'm really good with animals."

"Alice?" Adam whispered. "What about our mission?"

Alice grabbed Adam's arm and pulled him away. "Listen, Sharp! This is my one chance to be a star!" Alice said. "You saw me hypnotize those kangaroos! I'm good!"

"Alice," Adam said, "calm down."

Adam needed Alice so he could get over the fence when the mission was done. Or he needed Wayne's tunnel. Either way, he had to stick with these two.

"Okay," Adam said. "I'll help you make your movie."

"You can run the camera," Wayne told him. "Just aim it at me and Alice."

Adam nodded. He knew about cameras. But this one was much bigger than the one in his bow tie.

Adam held up the camera. "Ready . . . Action!" he cried.

Wayne and Alice started crawling on their stomachs toward the thornbush.

"I know you're in there, mate!" Wayne said. He turned to the camera and grinned. "If this three-fanged whippersnapper snake bites me, it's curtains for Wayne Wallaby."

Just then, a snake stuck its head out
from behind the thornbush.

Alice pointed her finger and stared at it.
In seconds, the snake was hypnotized.

Wayne grabbed the snake and held it up
to the camera. "Take a look at this little
beauty!" he said.

Suddenly, there was a loud whooshing noise above them.

Adam shined the spotlight into the night sky. It lit up a big red hot-air balloon.

"Alice!" Adam said. "The evil satellite balloon launch site must be somewhere around here!"

"Adam! We're making a movie!" Alice said. "You just ruined that shot!"

"Evil satellite balloon launch site?" Wayne repeated curiously.

Adam shined the spotlight back on Alice and Wayne. Uh-oh. Now he'd done it. He'd blown his cover.

"Wallaby, here's the deal. Alice and I

work for IM-8. We're secret agents," he said. "If you help us with our mission, I'll help you with your movie. I'll also ask IM-8 to free Alice from spying so she can be a star!"

Alice ran to Adam and hugged him.

"It's a deal, mate!" Wayne said. "If Alice can hypnotize dangerous snakes, I'll never get bitten again!"

They grabbed the spotlight and camera and jumped onto Wayne's motorcycle.

For the rest of the night, they ate trail mix and rode all over the Outback. But they didn't see any more hot-air balloons.

As the sun came up, they came to a big red rock. "Wow!" Adam said. "I've never seen a rock that big before . . . or that red!"

"It was part of Big Red Rock National Park. Now it's just a big red rock," Alice said. "We played on it all the time before the rancher put up the fence."

"I used to get bitten here a lot," Wayne said. "Hey, do you want to climb it, mate?"

Adam knew they really should look for the evil satellite balloon launch site. But he loved to climb. Especially big rocks.

"Okay," Adam said. "After all, we need to check out every inch of this ranch. The balloon launch site might be here."

Wayne stopped the motorcycle. Alice and Adam and Wayne got off. They started

climbing. It was just as fun as Adam knew
it would be.

All of a sudden, there was another loud
whooshing noise. A big red hot-air balloon
floated out of the top of the big red rock.

"Adam, you were right!" Alice looked at
him admiringly. "The big red rock is the
secret evil satellite balloon launch site!"

"It is?" Adam said. He was surprised. He hadn't really thought they'd find anything on the rock. "Oh, yes, right, um, yes! It is!" Adam recovered quickly.

Then they heard a voice yelling, "NO! NO! NO! They all have to go up at once! People will think it's a hot-air balloon race!"

"That voice came from *inside* the big red rock," Adam said.

Quickly, they climbed toward the top. But before they reached it, they had to stop. A big thornbush blocked their way.

Adam pulled apart the bush's branches. "There's a tunnel behind it!" he said.

5
Balloon Fight

Adam led the way. Stone steps went down and down and around and around. At the bottom, the tunnel opened into a huge room. Hundreds of soldiers were sitting on the floor blowing up big red hot-air balloons.

A neon sign hung from the ceiling. In red letters, it said: MENACE RADIO AND TV STATION. HAVE A HAPPY DAY!

"It's General Menace! My archenemy!" Adam clenched his fists. "I should have known he was behind the Happy Channel!"

"Let me at that little ripper!" Wayne said. *"Grrr!"*

Alice held him back. "No, Wayne!" she said. "This is a job for secret agents!"

Alice turned to Adam. "Blowing up big balloons is really hard work, mate," she said. "Why doesn't General Menace just send up regular rockets?"

"Simple, Alice," Adam said. "He knows that secret agencies don't worry about hot-air balloons."

Adam, Alice, and Wayne watched the

soldiers. After they finished blowing up a balloon, they tied a straw basket to the bottom with four big rubber bands.

"That must be where they put the evil satellites," Adam whispered. "The balloons carry them up into the sky, and they mess up the good satellites."

"Oh, that is so mean!" Alice said.

"We need to stop them. Otherwise the world will only see and hear what General Menace wants," Adam said. "I have an idea. Come on!"

They ran back up the stone steps. Adam pulled a lot of thorns off the thornbush.

"Here's the plan," he said. "Alice and I

will get into one of the straw baskets. Wayne, you untie the balloon, so that we will float up through the hole in the big red rock. We'll find all of General Menace's evil red satellite balloons and pop them out of the sky."

"Adam Sharp, no wonder you're IM-8's top agent!" Alice said.

Adam nodded. Sometimes it was hard to be humble. "Wayne, after we're in the air, you go back to the motorcycle and wait for us."

"Gotcha, mate!" Wayne said.

They ran down the stone steps. Adam and Alice climbed inside a straw basket. Wayne untied the rope, and the balloon

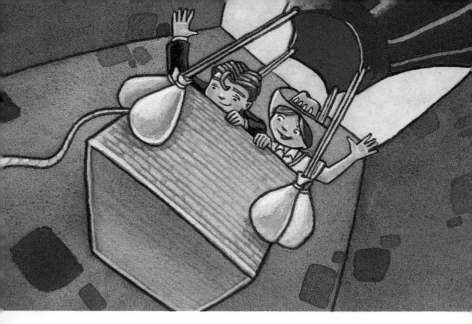

floated toward the top of the big red rock.

All of a sudden, General Menace yelled,
"HEY! STOP THAT BALLOON!"

Adam and Alice peeked over the basket
and waved at General Menace.

"The Happy Channel is going off the
air!" Adam shouted. "It's history!"

"Yeah!" Alice shouted. "The Happy

Channel is now the *history* channel!"

"Adam Sharp and Alice Springs!"
General Menace cried. He shook his fist
at them. "I'll get you for this!"

General Menace ran over to a balloon
and jumped into the straw basket.

"He's following us!" Adam said.

Their balloon squeezed out of the top
of the rock. Up, up, up they went. And so
did General Menace.

"We have to work fast!" Adam said.
"Look! There's a satellite balloon!"

Adam untied the bottom of his balloon.
He let out a burst of air. The balloon took
off like a jet plane. Luckily, Adam knew

how to handle it. He had trained as a jet pilot.

They flew right next to the satellite balloon. Alice stuck it with a thorn. The balloon popped and fell to the ground.

"It works, mate!" Alice shouted. She scanned the sky. "There's another one!"

Adam flew toward it. But General Menace reached the balloon first.

"He won't let us get close enough so you can pop it," Adam said.

"No problem, mate!" Alice said. "Watch this!"

She pulled back one of the big rubber bands and put a thorn against it like a bow

with an arrow. The thorn flew through the air
and struck the balloon. POP!

"Good work, Alice!" Adam shouted. "Now
let's complete this mission!"

Adam flew toward the other balloons.
General Menace was right behind them. But
Adam did a couple of loop-the-loops and
outsmarted him.

Alice shot thorns at the hot-air balloons. They all popped. But as the last one fell, General Menace caught up. He crashed into their balloon. "It's over for you, Adam Sharp!" General Menace shouted. "Your show has been canceled! Heh! Heh! Heh!"

The crash knocked Adam out of the straw basket. At the last second, he grabbed the side. He was hanging on by his fingertips.

Adam and Alice's balloon tilted crazily. Alice jumped to the other side of the basket to balance it. Adam gritted his teeth.

He pulled himself back into the basket. It was just like doing chin-ups in spy training.

"That was close!" Adam said. He looked at Alice. "There's only one thorn and one balloon left. You know what to do!"

Alice grinned. She fired the thorn at General Menace's balloon.

It missed and struck General Menace instead. "Ouch!" he cried.

"Oops!" Alice called. "Sorry!"

General Menace pulled out the thorn. He

gave Adam and Alice an evil grin. "Heh! Heh! Heh!" he laughed loudly.

General Menace put the thorn against a rubber band, pulled it back, and shot it toward Adam and Alice's balloon.

Adam kept his eye on the thorn as it headed toward them. At the last second, he turned the balloon so that the thorn hit one of their rubber bands. It bounced off and flew back toward General Menace's balloon.

There was a loud pop.

General Menace and the straw basket fell to earth.

"See you on the *Un*happy Channel!" Adam shouted. He checked the sky for balloons. "Our work here is done," he said.

Adam set a course for the big red rock. Alice kept watch over the side.

"I see Wayne's motorcycle!" Alice said.

A few seconds later, they landed. Adam looked around. The ground was covered with the balloons Alice had popped.

"Adam!" Alice said. "Look!"

General Menace and his soldiers were standing on top of the big red rock.

General Menace had on a parachute. He was shaking his fist at Adam and Alice. The soldiers looked out of breath.

Alice and Adam ran over to Wayne's motorcycle. Adam turned on the radio.

"You're listening to the Top Forty hits on Radio Australia," a voice said. "We're glad to be back on the air."

Adam grinned at Alice. "The world is normal again," he said.

Alice nodded. "Until General Menace thinks up something else mean to do, mate!" she said.

"Now what?" Wayne said.

"That's easy," Adam said. He picked up the movie camera. "Places, everyone. And . . . *action!*"